For my husband and children. You are my inspiration.
I love you.

Mommy, Am I Brown?
Paperback ISBN 978-0-578-48253-8

Written by Deandra Abuto
Illustrated by Mileidy Fernandez

Mommy, am I Brown?

This Book Belongs To:

Deandra Abuto illustrated by Mileidy Fernandez

"Ice cream," Eli said. He ran to the ice cream stand.
"I love chocolate!" He looked at his favorite flavor.

He jumped with joy when the giant chocolate scoop was placed on top. He stared at the tower of flavors.

"Mommy, am I brown?"
Eli asked.

"Sweetheart, you are brown,"
she replied.

"Mommy, am I smart?" he wondered.

"Eli, you are smart," she said.

"Mommy, am I brave?" Eli asked.

"Yes, you are brave. You can touch the moon and stars. You are the twinkling light that reaches beyond to Mars," she said.

"Mommy, am I loved?" Eli asked.
She wrapped her arms around him.
"You are loved. Your heart is big and
bold. Your smile sparkles like gold."

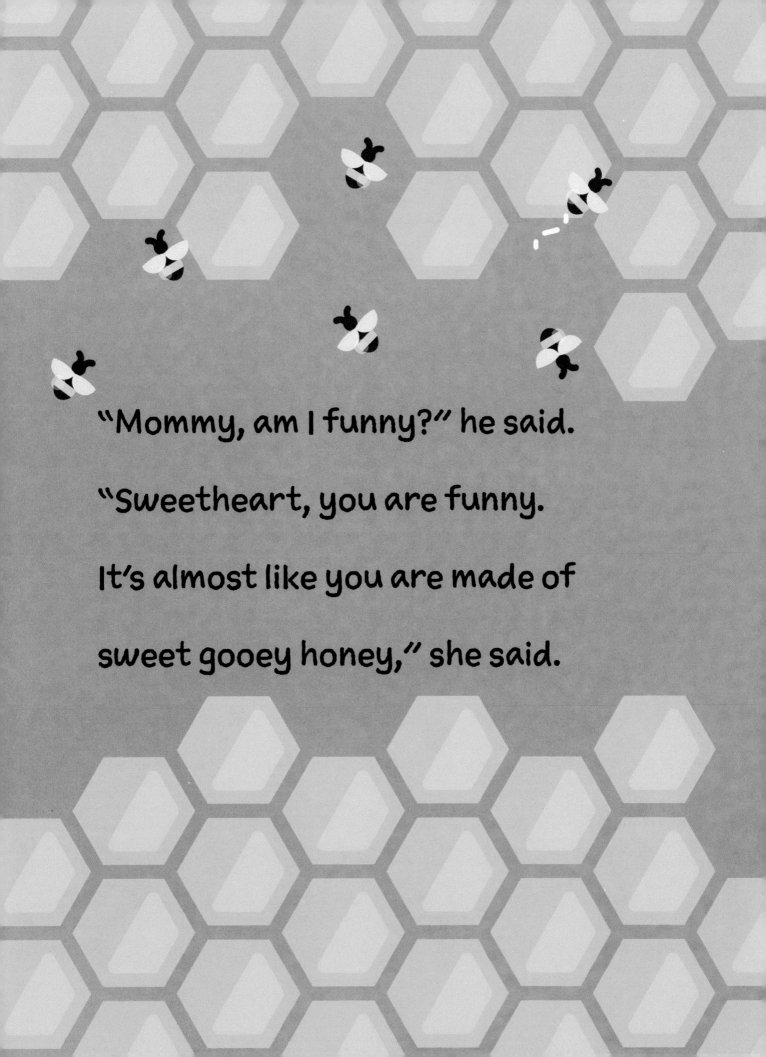

"Mommy, am I funny?" he said.

"Sweetheart, you are funny.

It's almost like you are made of

sweet gooey honey," she said.

"Mommy, am I brown?" he said.

"Eli, your skin is beautiful and brown. Your soul is a rainbow that is made from many colors," she replied.

Eli looked up to the sky.
"Mommy, am I yellow?"

"You are yellow. You are the sunlight
that shines across the mountains
and the seas," she replied.

He touched the sand. "Am I orange?"
"You are the joy that comes with the
morning light," she said.

"Mommy, am I red?" he asked. "Yes, sweetheart, your heart is red," she said.

"Am I purple?" he said. "Purple will help you reach your dreams wherever you are," she said.

Eli laid down in the grass. "Am I green?" he said. "Green is the earth which is a part of you," she answered.

"Mommy, am I blue?" he asked.

"You are blue. Blue is your power that spreads across the skies," she said.

Eli held up the stuff animal.
"Mommy, am I strong?"

She smiled at him.
"Yes, you are."

Eli kicked the soccer ball
around the park. "Look at me."

Eli thought about the day.

He turned to his mother. "Mommy, I am..."

"Eli, sweetheart....
Yes, you are."

Deandra Abuto is a former middle school English teacher. Helping children learn the joy of reading continues to be her passion. She lives with her husband and children in Texas.

Mileidy Fernández is an illustrator from Venezuela.

Made in the USA
Middletown, DE
04 July 2019